The Apprentice

THE

APPRENTICE .

PILAR MOLINA LLORENTE

Pictures by Juan Ramón Alonso

TRANSLATED BY ROBIN LONGSHAW

FARRAR, STRAUS AND GIROUX

NEW YORK

Text copyright © 1989 by Pilar Molina Llorente
Pictures copyright © 1989 by Juan Ramón Alonso
English translation copyright © 1993 by Farrar, Straus and Giroux
Originally published in Spanish by Ediciones Rialp, S.A.,
under the title *El aprendiz*
All rights reserved
Library of Congress catalog card number: 92-54648
Published simultaneously in Canada by HarperCollins*CanadaLtd*
Printed in the United States of America
Designed by Debbie Glasserman
First American edition, 1993

for Rubén

Preface

During the Renaissance, which lasted from the fifteenth through the seventeenth century, the world witnessed an artistic movement out of which emerged some of mankind's greatest creative achievements. Michelangelo's statue of David, Brunelleschi's cupola, and Botticelli's *Primavera* are but a few of the masterpieces that survive as a testament to this rebirth of classical ideas and influences from ancient Rome and Greece.

Florence, Italy, was the cultural capital of this world. Its system of patronage encouraged a spirit of civic competitiveness and pride, motivating an impressive number of painters, sculptors, and architects to adorn their city. Most noteworthy among the wealthy patrons was the ruling

Medici family, which for several generations commissioned hundreds of works of art.

Despite this ideal atmosphere, the artist's job was never an easy one. Behind every masterpiece were long hours of hard work, anguish, even disappointment. In the story that follows, a young Florentine boy, Arduino, dreams of becoming a painter and taking on whatever challenges that may bring. The first is to become a painter's apprentice.

Every Renaissance artist had his or her beginnings, and in many ways Arduino's story, though fictional, is a window on that world—on the everyday hardships, as well as the occasional triumphs, experienced by many a struggling young artist of the time.

The Apprentice

Chapter One

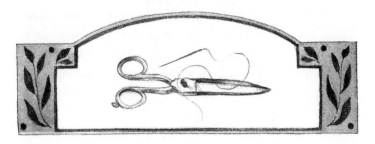

My house was a small and pleasant one. It had a court-yard with a bronze fountain in the shape of a fish's head and a tall gallery, full of light and flowers. What I liked best about it, though, was the large window in the gallery that opened onto the square and the bustling outdoor market. I sat at that window nearly every morning, before I went to work in my father's tailor shop, and tried to draw the postures and gestures of the vendors in their stalls and the expressions of their customers. Again and again I realized that no one has the same nose as anyone else and that each person has a different way of walking.

One morning, I stayed later than usual at the gallery window. My father's voice brought me back from my world of lines and shadings and dropped me roughly into the reality of the workday.

"Arduino, are you going to spend the whole morning at the window? There's work to be done." He was standing at the gallery door.

I put down my paper and pencil and followed him toward the tailor's shop, which was part of our house. There, day after day, my grandfather, my father, my brothers, and I put in the thousands of stitches that together formed each piece and then the finished garments. The clicking of the needles against the thimbles counted the seconds.

In the shop, my brothers were finishing up a pair of breeches. I found some basting that I had begun the day before, and sat down to sew. I looked at my father, who had resumed his work at the cutting table. His hands moved with the agility of a magician's as he folded the silk in two, right sides together, and then rapidly marked four or five measurements that would serve as guidelines for cutting the fabric with his huge black scissors. He glanced up and saw me looking at him, then frowned and called me over. He motioned me toward the back of the shop, away from the others.

"Son," he said sternly, "you haven't been concentrating on your work. You can't even get simple hems straight."

"It's hard for me, Father."

"Hard? At your age your brother Antonio was already embroidering doublets with pearls."

"But Antonio—" I started to say.

"Antonio pays attention to what he is doing and nothing else. You, on the other hand, your head is full of drawing and sketching nonsense—you spend so much time at that window. You're thirteen now. You should be refining your tailoring skills, not ignoring them. This is your opportunity to become a master. Do you know what the word 'master' means?"

"Yes, but . . ."

"But what?"

I felt trapped. I had to tell him the truth, for my father always knew by looking in my eyes if I was lying.

"It's just that, for me, being a tailor is . . . is . . ."

My father's face was redder than usual and it frightened me.

"I don't like tailoring," I said, all in a rush.

My father stiffened. "You don't like it," he said. "Tailoring is your family trade. It is what your great-grandfather and your grandfather have done. It is what I do and it is what your brothers do. We have illustrious clients who know us and place their trust in us. The whole city respects our name. Do you think you could go as far in another trade?"

He was right. My father was proud of the place he had in society and of the way people, even outside Florence, spoke of his good taste, his skill with the scissors, his hard work, and his sense of honor. But it wasn't for me.

"I want to be a painter," I finally dared to say, and my own voice sounded strange to me.

"A painter? Do you know how difficult it is to become

established as a painter? There are many young men who want to be artists—how many succeed?"

"I will," I said, with as much conviction as I could muster.

My father watched me in silence. His eyes were trying to read in mine the seriousness of my intentions.

"Very well," he said gravely. "I will speak with Cosimo di Forlì. He has an important studio and he owes me a favor or two."

I knelt down and kissed my father's hand over and over. I couldn't think of any other way to show him how grateful I was.

"Listen, Arduino," he said. "You will have only one chance. If Cosimo di Forlì tells me that you have no future as a painter, or if he has any complaint about your behavior, you will come home to be a tailor like your brothers. Do you understand?"

I nodded. The knot in my throat kept me from speaking.

The following day, my father left the shop to meet with Maestro Cosimo di Forlì. I knew that I was the subject of their discussion, and each moment my father was gone seemed to last an eternity. When he finally returned, he brought good news. The Maestro had agreed to take me on as an apprentice, and I could go as soon as I was ready.

My father said I would go in five days. That would give me enough time to finish up my work in the shop, to prepare what I would take with me, and to say goodbye to my friends from other shops around the square. Depending on the terms of the apprenticeship, which would be finalized on my arrival at the Maestro's house, I might not be returning home for a while.

My brothers said I was crazy. They were very happy to be tailors. Antonio, the oldest, loved fabrics and embroideries; he knew their textures with his eyes closed, and the perfect drape of a piece of silk or the combination of colors in a cape gave him great satisfaction.

Tailoring was ideal for Enzo, three years older than me, because it was a respectable trade that allowed him to work at home and did not require him to exercise his legs, thin and twisted after a childhood illness. Antonio and Enzo both laughed at my dreams and tried to convince me that I was making a mistake.

I listened respectfully to their advice and criticism, but at night, with my elbows on the ledge of the gallery window, I gazed at the tiny patch of stars over the empty square and knew in my heart that I was right. I wanted to learn the secrets of shapes and colors and somehow to express my feelings about beautiful and interesting people and things. My brothers' words seemed less sensible when set against the strength of my dreams. But in the back of my mind there was that shadow of fear—the fear of failure and of the unknown that had always haunted me.

The day I was to leave dawned so cold the rooster's crow almost froze in his throat. As soon as I heard his strangled cry, I jumped out of bed and began to dress. I hadn't slept all night from anticipation and now I was so nervous I tore one of my stockings.

When it was time to go I bid my grandfather and my brothers farewell at least three times and checked over the satchel my father had made from some leftover cloth to hold my belongings. After one last goodbye to my old dog, Nero, Father and I were on our way.

Cosimo di Forlì lived on the other side of the city, in an old neighborhood with narrow streets and dark, mysterious-looking doorways. As we walked, my father was silent and thoughtful. I was nervous and impatient. To calm myself, I tried to think of my mother, who died so long ago that I could barely remember her face. At times, my faint memory of her gave me some comfort. Then, in my mind's eye, I said goodbye to the courtyard, the fountain, the outdoor market, and the workshop. I realized that I was truly leaving behind the Arduino from before: the tailor's son.

The Maestro's house had a decayed façade and a door knocker in the shape of a lion's head. A very large, middle-aged woman answered our knock, her figure filling the doorway.

"What do you want?" she said, frowning.

My father introduced himself and explained why he had come, and the woman moved to one side.

"Please come in," she said in a friendlier tone. "The Maestro will be with you in a minute."

We followed her into a dark, quiet room. She told us to wait, then disappeared behind a curtain. There was a little light coming from under the curtain, but as I looked around, the room was so dark I could see only the outlines of a table and a bench. The walls were nearly invisible in the shadows, and I couldn't tell if the shapes in the corners were chests or shelves.

The silence was interrupted by the sound of someone clearing his throat. I turned quickly and saw a hand pull the curtain aside. There, in the dim light, was a short, stocky man, wearing a dun-colored cap with pieces of his gray hair sticking out from under it. It was the Maestro.

He stepped into the room, letting the curtain fall behind him. He squinted, and examined me from head to toe, pausing a moment when he arrived at my eyes.

"Well, well. This is the boy," he said in a hoarse voice.

"Arduino di Emilio di Antonio Neri," said my father, presenting me formally.

"Arduino," said the Maestro. "Let's see what you can do. Melania!"

The woman—Melania—came out from behind the curtain and stood in front of it, blocking with her skirt the light that came from beneath it.

"Melania," said the Maestro, "bring us a sheet of paper and a candle."

She nodded and left the room, returning a moment later

with the paper and a lit candle, which she set carefully on the table. The Maestro took a charcoal pencil from one of his pockets and handed it to me. "Draw a circle," he said.

I could feel my knees shaking as I stood there. Nobody had said anything about a test! My performance now might decide my future as a painter. It isn't as easy as it seems to draw a perfect circle; I knew it was the test of a steady hand, common in workshops, and is often a dare among the boys who work there. I was sure of my ability—I had drawn hundreds of circles—but I was not so sure of my nerves. I took a deep breath and drew. The circle was nearly perfect.

Cosimo di Forlì looked at it and nodded. He pushed his gray hair back from his temples.

"Let us draw up the contract," he said to my father.

I breathed a sigh of relief.

"Now, Arduino," he said, "you may draw what you like."

I turned the paper over and thought. I had drawn my grandfather's hands on the head of his walking stick so many times that I had memorized their relaxed lines and the shadows that told the tale of many years of hard work. I sat down on the wobbly bench next to the table and tried to concentrate on the picture, as I listened to their conversation.

Cosimo was dictating the contract that would bind me to him. As was the custom in a painter's workshop, I would live with Cosimo di Forlì for the next three years, serving him not only in his painting but in whatever he should ask, obeying his orders, and following his every instruction. The

first year, my father would pay for my apprenticeship. From the second year on, the Maestro would pay me a salary in proportion to my skills, which he would determine. I finished my drawing as they agreed on the last few details.

"Very well, Master Emilio," the Maestro was saying, "we agree on the conditions. I hope that the boy—"

He stopped when he saw my drawing. He took the sheet in his hands and studied it slowly. Then he raised his eyes and looked at me piercingly.

"What did you say your name was?"

"Arduino," I said. It came out as a whisper.

There was an awkward silence until finally my father spoke. "Very well, Cosimo. If at any time the boy misbehaves or slacks off in his work, send for me. I'll come right away. He is here against my wishes, and I need him at the shop, so at the slightest complaint he will leave painting and return to sewing."

This was addressed to me as much as to the Maestro.

"I will keep it in mind," said the Maestro, smiling, though in the flickering candlelight his smile seemed almost sinister.

My father came over to me, and I stood up from the table. "Remember," he said, "your actions reflect on our family, and everything that you do or say will come back to us. Remember that."

I nodded. He made the sign of the cross over me and left.

Chapter Two

When the door closed behind my father, I suddenly felt very alone and afraid.

"Come along," said the Maestro coldly.

The darkness of the room paralyzed me. The Maestro doesn't seem to be very friendly, I thought, but he isn't going to eat me. I have to—

"Come on! Are you hard of hearing or just stupid?" he barked. I grabbed my satchel, and he pushed me into a narrow hallway just behind the curtain.

The hallway led to a smallish room with two doors, one of which opened onto the kitchen. The other door was closed. There was a stone staircase in the corner.

"Melania!" yelled the Maestro.

A damp smell from the terra-cotta tiles that covered the

floor stuck in my throat. I set the satchel down at my feet.

"Melania!" he yelled again, louder.

The sound of halting steps announced her arrival.

"Coming, coming," she said in a deep voice. Then, as if to herself, she added, "Someday that beast will wear out my name.

"Well, what is it?" she said, standing in the doorway that we had just come in.

"Prepare lodging for this boy."

Melania hit her hip with her hand, and a cloud of dust or flour escaped from her skirt.

"Another boy? There's no room for another in the sleeping quarters. They'll suffocate in there."

With his foot, the Maestro pushed my satchel into the middle of the room.

"Here, take his things. Make a place for him where you can, and don't give me any more problems than I already have."

Melania abruptly picked up the bundle, gave him a look, and walked away, muttering, "Problems, problems. His only problem is his bad temper."

Shaking his head, the Maestro walked over to the closed door and opened it. A stream of light filled the room.

"Go in," he said.

It was the studio. There were tables, easels, benches . . . a real studio! Three boys were working in the room —also apprentices, I guessed. They all looked up from what they were doing as we entered the room.

"Piero!" the Maestro called to a boy working at one of

the tables. "Give Arduino an apron and show him how to prepare pigments."

I took a deep breath and tried to convince myself that I was just shivering from the cold.

Piero was much taller than I, pale and thin. He looked at me without much interest and handed me a stiff, dirty apron. Then he showed me to a table with rows of flasks containing colored earths and bowls with greases and liquids.

"Take the mortar and pestle and crush these chunks until you have very fine powder," he said. "When it's completely ground, put it in here." He pointed to a bowl.

I picked up the heavy pestle and began to grind the green-colored earth. Some pieces flew out of the mortar.

"Don't thump so hard, and use more precision," Piero explained, "and be careful, because the powder is very poisonous."

I began again, this time with better results. Piero returned to his work, and I continued quietly, enjoying the regular grinding rhythm of pestle against mortar.

After a while, one of the other boys in the studio came over to my table, put on an apron, and took a mortar. He was heavyset and had a red nose. We worked in silence. In the huge room, the only sounds were the syncopated clicks and thumps of the mortars and pestles. Suddenly he spoke.

"How old are you?" he asked.

"I'm going on fourteen," I answered.

"Hah! I'm fifteen." He smirked and then chuckled to himself, as though the fact that he was a year older was very

funny indeed. Then he blurted out, "I am Baldo Ferruccio. I'm Antonio Ferruccio's grandson."

I felt a flash of envy. Antonio Ferruccio was a famous painter of altarpieces. For Baldo, it would surely be simple to become a painter.

Before I had a chance to say anything, the Maestro called me over to his table. He was holding a small drawing.

"Tell me, what do you think of this?" he asked.

The picture was a sepia pencil drawing of five figures: three women and two children. The composition of the figures, the balance of the shapes, and the complexity of the light and shadow were extraordinary. But at that moment, I couldn't speak; I could only feel a white heat that seemed to imprint the vision in my brain. I had felt that way before when looking at a painting, the arch of a church, my grandfather's face in the firelight . . .

"Well," said the Maestro, "I'm beginning to think you really are hard of hearing. I asked you what you thought of this drawing."

"It's very . . . very beautiful," I stammered.

"Do you recognize the subject?"

I couldn't think. I shook my head.

"You're religious, aren't you?"

"Yes."

"Yes, Maestro," he corrected me. "Look, this is Saint Anne, here is Saint Elizabeth, and on the right, Our Lady, the Virgin Mary."

He was staring at me. I nodded. "And the children?" he asked.

"Baby Jesus and Saint John the Baptist."

"Very good, very good. Perhaps you have more in your head than brocades and baubles." He began to laugh, but then his laughter turned into a rude cough that forced him to leave the studio.

When I returned to the mortar, I saw that the green earth was strewn over the table, and that the powder I had ground was laced with black earth and pebbles.

Baldo's smothered giggles told me that this was a prank reserved for the new boy in the studio.

"It was you," I said to him.

Baldo snickered.

"What's so funny? You must think you're very clever. Well, you're not! You're a fool, a clown, a—"

"What's going on here!" roared the Maestro from the doorway.

I thought quickly. If I told him what had happened, the other boys would hate me. And I did have to live with them for the next three years.

"It's nothing," I answered. "I was distracted, and I mixed the pigments by accident."

The Maestro shuffled over to the worktable and examined the mess.

"What waste," he grumbled. His mouth, missing some teeth, let fly little drops of spit. "These earths are expensive, especially the green, which is scarce. You can't just throw them around. Now, save what you can and clean up the rest. Don't let it happen again!"

He walked away muttering.

When Cosimo was out of earshot, I said to Baldo, "Don't you ever play another trick on me! I don't want the Maestro to think I'm careless!"

Baldo snorted in response.

I spent the rest of that first morning grinding pigments and putting up with the laughter that Baldo seemed to be holding back between his cheeks and his nose.

We stopped working to eat lunch. The meal was a thin broth with strange pieces of meat that Melania, groaning and complaining, served in earthenware bowls on the greasy kitchen table.

Back in the studio, the afternoon passed in much the same way as the morning. When the light began to fade in the studio, we left our work and returned to the kitchen for evening chores.

"Someone needs to fetch the water," said Piero.

"Let Arduino get it. The new boy always gets it." It was Marco, the boy who had been working at an easel in the back of the workshop. From his tone of voice, I knew I didn't have a choice.

Outside, it was very cold. The autumn wind cut through my thin doublet. When I got to the well, I lowered the bucket carefully. At home, I had never been allowed to get water from the well. It was considered too dangerous for me, the youngest, though I knew how it was done from watching my father. When I figured the bucket was full, I began to pull on the rope. I could barely budge it.

"Let me help you," came a voice from behind me. It was Piero.

It was a difficult job even for the two of us. After much heaving and straining, we were finally able to rest the bucket on the edge of the well.

When we returned to the house, we joined Baldo and Marco for the rest of the chores. We got wood for the hearth, shuttered the windows, cleaned the stable, and groomed the Maestro's aged horse. Exhausted, we trudged back to the kitchen for supper. Melania set out bowls of bread and milk.

We all ate to the accompaniment of Baldo's slurps and stories that Melania told us in hushed tones about the demons, devils, and crazed criminals that wandered the streets. I soon learned that her storytelling was a regular event at suppertime. Despite their morbid topics, the stories took our minds off the cold drafts around our ankles and the meager food.

When we were through eating, we helped Melania wash the dishes and headed off to bed. I still felt hungry, though I didn't ask for more. It was my first day, and I didn't want the others to think I was greedy.

Piero, Baldo, and Marco slept in a room that was barely big enough for the three of them, so, for my bed, Melania had put down a straw pallet and a blanket on the floor underneath the stone staircase, where it wouldn't be in the way.

I lay down. I could smell straw dust, and the blanket stank of sweat and damp. I tried not to think of the sheets on my bed at home, which were always scented with mint.

Melania had put out the candle in the kitchen, so the

room was nearly dark. Moonlight slid through the cracks in the shutters of the small window on the far wall. Though I was tired, the newness of my surroundings kept me awake. I could hear the mice scratching behind the wall and other unknown noises that seemed to come from above. I went over the thousands of details of the day, which made me temporarily forget my hunger and cold. Finally I began to drift off, thinking of the marvelous drawing the Maestro had shown me. I was in this near-sleep state when I felt a human presence near me. I was wide awake in an instant, though I didn't move a muscle.

I heard soft footsteps. I opened my eyes as wide as I could, straining to see into the darkness, but from where I lay, it was hopeless. Whoever it was began to climb the stairs, carefully, so as not to make any noise.

I slowly sat up to get a better look and saw, thanks to the light coming through the cracks in the shutters, Melania, tiptoeing up the stairs with a bundle in one hand and a pail in the other. After a while, she came down with the same care and disappeared into the kitchen.

Who or what was upstairs? And why did Melania go there in the middle of the night?

I tossed and turned for a while, wondering about what I'd just witnessed. Finally, exhaustion got the better of me, and I fell into a fitful sleep.

Chapter Three

It was a cold day. Breakfast, a thick and sticky porridge, left me feeling sluggish. The only thing I wanted was to get into the studio, where it was warm and bright. Along with the other boys, I had finished the morning chores; Baldo and I had scrubbed the kitchen floor with water and sand. Now we fidgeted, waiting for the Maestro to finish his meal.

With a final gulp of his hot wine, he stood up from the kitchen table. He stuffed his dirty locks under his cap and ambled out of the kitchen to the studio. We all got up and followed him, including Melania. When he opened the door, the light in the room was blinding.

Baldo and Piero walked to a table, put on their aprons, and began to work with the mortars and pigments. I started toward them.

"Arduino, you come here." Melania's voice was firm. She held a broom toward me. I hesitated.

"Well, come on. What are you waiting for? Saint George isn't going to come down from heaven to save you from the job. Sweep everything well, especially the corners."

The broom was heavy and rough with splinters. I dragged it to the farthest end of the studio first and began to sweep. Little black spiders ran from every nook and cranny. There were even a few swinging from the beams. I decided that the only time the studio was cleaned was when a new boy arrived.

"Hey, be careful!" Marco yelled.

Without meaning to, I had hit the leg of his easel with the broom.

"I'm sorry," I said and stopped sweeping. I watched him spread blue oil paint over the background of his painting.

"What are you looking at?" he said, his eyes still on the canvas. "Don't you have anything better to do than bother everyone else?"

"I . . . was just watching."

"Watching? As if you know what you're looking at!"

His haughty tone made me flush with anger. Of course I knew!

"I was watching you work," I answered firmly. "That background is too strong. The sky is never that blue."

He spun to face me, furious. "Just who do you think you're talking to?" he shouted. "You're nothing but a child. You have no right to correct me! How dare you!"

The Maestro came over, grumbling. "Another fight? Arduino, your father didn't say anything about your bad temper."

"I don't have a bad temper," I protested. "But everyone here seems to think—"

The Maestro interrupted me, raising his hoarse voice. "The only thing that matters here is what I think. Keep sweeping if you don't want me to talk to your father about your behavior."

He mentioned my father to scare me, and it worked. I would have to put up with whatever came my way, no matter how difficult or insulting it might be. What was really important was learning to paint, recognizing the materials, knowing the techniques. If I ever got the chance!

I took up the broom again and began to sweep, my eyes burning. The Maestro spoke again, this time to Marco. His tone of voice startled me.

"This background color will never work! Think of the intensity of the light and the colors that we are going to give the figures. The background of a composition like this one requires a detailed study of tones and shades. You should know that by now, Marco. You can't just put color on a canvas without defining it first." He sighed deeply as if he had said something of great importance. "Now, clean off the excess paint and prepare a more appropriate shade of blue."

I was right! The satisfaction I felt helped me finish my work in a much better mood than the one I had started in.

. . .

"Arduino, bring me some water!"

"Hey, boy, get me that board!"

"Get out of the way! Don't bother me!"

All day long, I ran back and forth, following orders and fetching things. I helped in the kitchen and in the henhouse, drew water from the well and chopped firewood, straightened a twisted bellows, shook out a threadbare blanket, and shined the knocker on the front door. Finally, when I thought I could do no more, it was time for supper.

I joined the other boys, who were seated at the warm kitchen hearth, eating thick soup and a chunk of bacon. Marco got up as soon as he'd finished eating, so just Baldo, Piero, and I were left sitting there. I watched Melania's enormous cat, who ruled the kitchen secure in his place as the mistress's favorite. I thought of Melania's midnight excursion up the stairs.

I looked at Baldo, who was eating his bacon with gusto, and Piero, who was taking the last sips of his soup.

"Do either of you know what's in the attic?" I asked.

Baldo started, then whispered urgently, "I've never been up there, and I never would go up there. And neither should you. The Maestro would get very angry!"

"Of course I don't want the Maestro to get angry. I just want to know what's up there," I whispered back. I decided not to reveal what I'd seen the night before.

"The Maestro doesn't want anyone to go up that staircase. He gets furious and Melania growls like a lion whenever anyone even asks about the attic."

"Why?"

"We don't know," Baldo said in such a low voice that I could barely hear him. "They say that . . ."

"What?" I asked impatiently.

"That the Maestro has a dead body hidden up there."

"A dead body? Whose?"

"Nobody knows."

A shiver traveled up my back and to the very ends of my fingers.

Piero, who had been listening in silence to our conversation, spoke without taking his eyes from the fire in the hearth.

"A boy who was here when I arrived said that the Maestro kept a strange wild beast from Africa up in the attic. He said that he had heard hair-raising cries and groans."

"That's horrible!"

"Anyway, I think . . ."

"Yes?"

Piero looked toward the table where the Maestro was going over his account ledger and then at the corner where Marco, far from the rest of us, was studying the fret board of his lute. Convinced that no one else would hear him, he continued. "I think there is an alchemist's or wizard's laboratory up there. The Maestro knows a lot about minerals and liquids, and sometimes he has very strange visitors."

"Maybe they're just traveling merchants who sell rare pigments and works of art," said Baldo.

Piero looked skeptical. "Then why do they always seem to be hiding something?"

Baldo shrugged. "They work illegally. They probably sell stolen goods. That's why they're so mysterious."

The two spoke calmly, as though the subject had nothing to do with them, as though whatever there was upstairs was miles away, instead of right over our heads. I was sweating, in spite of the cold draft that came in through the cracks in the windows and doors.

Baldo and Piero went on whispering about the mystery in the attic and Cosimo's odd activities until Melania walked by us to hang some pots on their hooks. The subject was changed to Baldo's favorite—food.

Later, lying in bed, I heard Melania go upstairs again. Afterward, there were strange creaking and scraping noises that seemed to come from the attic.

If there was a dead body, I thought, why would Melania bother going up there? Besides, dead bodies don't make noise. An alchemist's laboratory isn't noisy either, especially if no one is using it—the Maestro never goes up there. Unless Melania . . . but no, she's barely up there five minutes at a time. The only possibility is that there is a monster up there, or some strange animal, as Piero said. But why would the Maestro have something like that in the attic?

All I wanted to do was run away. But where would I go? Out into the cold, dark streets, which Melania said were full of criminals? I want to go home, I thought.

But if I went home, it would be forever—I would have no second chance. It meant going back to the needle and thread, back to basting and hemming, and fringing silks and

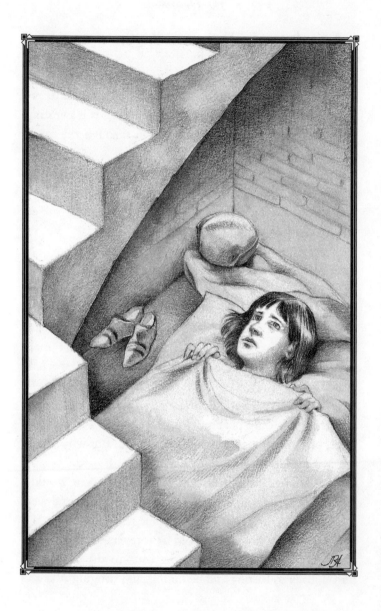

tying ribbons. And what about painting? Where had my dream of being a painter gone? It all seemed distant now, as if those dreams were someone else's.

My head was pounding as though a stone were rolling around inside it, and my trembling turned into tears.

Later, rolled tightly in my blanket, I realized that I had to make a decision, and there were only two paths: to leave this horrible monster-filled house and be a tailor, surrounded by comfort but bitter from failure; or to overcome my fears and all the difficulties of life here, and pursue the dreams that had grown within me on those many mornings at the gallery window.

Perhaps because day was breaking, or because I was tired of feeling sorry for myself, I decided to fight my fears and go on with the life I had chosen for myself. I would also try to find out what—or who—was upstairs.

Chapter Four

During the days that followed, light and work filled my thoughts, but when the shadows began to dull the colors of the paintings in the studio, and Melania began to shout about wasting oil and candles, so that we would hurry to bed, I was overcome by an anguish that washed over me like a wave. It seemed pointless to ask more questions about the attic. The other boys knew less than I did—they didn't even seem to care. In order to find out what was up there, I would have to go on my own, and it would have to be at night. It was impossible to linger near the stairway during the day. If the Maestro wasn't with us in the studio, we were never far from Melania's watchful gaze.

It wasn't long before I decided, one night, to carry out my investigation. The moon was full, and everyone was sleeping—Melania had made her silent visit to the attic an hour or so earlier. The only sounds in the house were the familiar popping of the last logs on the fire and the Maestro's snore, which echoed through the corridor. It was time to go upstairs.

I got up quietly and waited to be sure that no one had heard me. I stepped away from the corner that served as my bedroom and stood at the bottom of the stairway.

There were five steps that led to a small landing; then the staircase turned up to the attic. I held on to the rope that, anchored to the wall, served as a banister, and slowly began to climb the stairs. I reached the first landing and peered through the shadows. I could make out another landing at the top and a large door just beyond it.

When I reached the top, I leaned against the wall and took a deep breath. I had the sensation that my ears had grown, straining to hear any sounds.

The door was black and studded with rusted nailheads. I held the latch down and pushed, but the door was locked. I tried looking through the keyhole, but it seemed to be blocked, or covered from the other side.

I was thinking about giving up when a shuffling sound made me jump. I grabbed on to the rope banister and considered running downstairs as fast as I could, yelling until I had awakened the whole household. Something held me back.

I took another deep breath, and turned to examine the wall next to the door. Something near the floor, to the right of the door, moved in the shadows. I held my breath. My heartbeat seemed loud enough to wake all of Florence. I bent down to get a closer look. It looked like a piece of fabric. I touched it. It was heavy, like a tapestry. But why was it moving?

I mopped my brow and swallowed hard. Very slowly, I pulled back a corner of the tapestry and saw, about a foot off the floor, a small barred window that opened onto a room silvered by moonlight. The air that came through the bars smelled of acid dampness. I sat down on the floor and peered through the bars. The attic was a large, empty room with a barred window, which was open, letting in the moonlight and the cold of the street. There were no shelves or cupboards with alchemist's equipment against the walls, nor were there books or even a table or bench. I saw no bodies, ghosts, or dragons, just a pail, a dish, some rags, and, on the wall, a huge black iron ring and chain that reached a bundle of tattered blankets on the floor. The bundle was breathing.

Mother of God, I thought.

I tried to move, but my legs seemed to have stuck themselves to the floor. It was then that I heard a soft voice.

"Who are you?"

"Arduino," I answered.

The bundle had spoken! It was a man! He pushed aside the blanket that covered his head, and the moonlight shone on his hair.

"Good . . . good night," I stammered and dropped the tapestry.

"Wait!" he cried.

I couldn't move.

"Arduino, please," he said, "please don't go."

His voice was that of a young man—only a few years older than me. I pulled back the tapestry again. He was sitting under the open window, against the wall. The chain I had seen stretched across the room ended in a shackle around his ankle.

"Thank you," he said when he saw me.

"You . . . you . . . I . . ." So many questions crowded my thoughts that I couldn't say anything clearly.

"Are you one of Cosimo's apprentices?" he asked.

"Yes."

"My name is Donato."

"Do . . . Donato?" My voice cracked. "Why are you chained up in here?"

"Because," he said, "I was foolish. Please, please tell me, how are things downstairs? I only see Melania, and she never speaks to me."

I shrugged my shoulders. "I've only been here for a week," I answered. "I don't know if things are going well or badly."

"Is there very much work?"

"Not really, though they are finishing a panel and there's a drawing in progress."

"There's nothing else?" he asked, sounding surprised.

"Not that I know of."

He leaned toward the barred window and pushed the hair out of his face.

"Is there a specialist in the studio?" he asked.

I had never heard of such a thing.

"I don't think so," I said.

He looked at me and smiled. "A specialist is an expert in one particular part of a painting. There are specialists in backgrounds, in hands, in the folds of tunics and hangings."

"I've never seen any specialists," I answered. "Marco does the backgrounds, and the Maestro paints the rest."

"Marco is still here!" he exclaimed softly. "What about Raffaello?"

"No, aside from me and Marco, there's only Baldo and Piero. There are four of us altogether."

"They're new since I've been up here. Raffaello probably ran away after I was imprisoned."

"Why are you chained up in there?" I asked again.

There was a pause before he spoke.

"The Maestro thought that I painted better than he did. I never felt that way—I thought he was a genius—but I wasn't clever enough to hide my talent. I had been his apprentice for three years and spoke openly about plans to open my own studio. He got hysterical when he heard about it. He couldn't bear the thought of competing with me for commissions. He said I was a traitor."

I couldn't believe my ears. Could the Maestro really be that jealous?

"How long have you been in here?" I asked.

Donato looked at some scratches on the wall near the iron ring.

"Fourteen months," he said, sighing.

"Fourteen months!" I was stunned. "How have you managed to stand it?"

"What else could I do?" he said. "At the beginning, I was desperate. I wouldn't eat what Melania brought up to me, but I was starving and nobody cared whether I ate or not. I yelled many times, but no one ever came. The wisest thing I could do was wait."

"What about the other boys?"

"Marco and I weren't exactly friends and Raffaello was quite timid. In any case, nobody sees, hears, or knows anything that Cosimo doesn't want him to. Even though you've only been here a short time, you should know that."

It was true. No one contradicted the Maestro: apprentices are legally bound to obey their masters.

"But what about your family?" I asked him. "Haven't they looked for you?"

Donato took a deep breath and began his story.

"I have no family left. I was an orphan when I came to Cosimo. Both my parents and my sister had died several months earlier from a fever that I somehow survived. My father was a merchant and made good money, so when he was alive, I was able to go to the best schools, where I studied art, the sciences, philosophy, and literature. But my father didn't have much savings, and when he died, most of what he did have was used to pay debts. I had always known that I wanted to be an artist, so after all the debts were paid, I used the money that was left for an apprenticeship."

He paused, then continued. "From the moment he had my money, Cosimo took full advantage of the fact that I was orphaned—he thought he owned me."

"I would never have been able to stand it for so long. I would have gone mad," I said.

"For a while, I thought I was going mad, too. But little by little, I realized that losing my mind was useless—so was feeling sorry for myself. I decided to adapt to the situation, which is the only reason I've survived as long as I have."

"But you must be so lonely . . ."

"I am very cold and hungry and lonely, and being lonely is the worst. But I also have time to think, and because of my window, I can see the sun and the moon and the birds. I even know when things are happening here in Florence."

"What do you mean? That window is so high up. You can't possibly see very much out of it."

"Of course not," Donato said. "But I knew when it was Christmas, because I could hear the noises of the market and smell the roasting meats, and I knew when it was Carnival, because I heard the songs and the children shouting. San Lorenzo's bells tell me when it's Sunday, or when there's a wedding, or a funeral, or a fire."

He paused and wiped his face with the back of his hand. "I've even managed to get used to living with spiders and mice."

"Ugh! I'd have died of fright," I said.

"Fright?" Donato looked at me with surprise.

"Sometimes I think I'm a terrible coward," I said.

The prisoner shifted against the wall. He sighed and said softly, "You are the only boy who's dared to come up here in fourteen months. I don't believe you are a coward, even though you say so yourself."

"I'm still shaking."

"That doesn't mean anything."

The moon, indifferent to our conversation, had moved across the sky, and now only a sliver of light came through the open window.

"It's getting very late," I said. "I should go down to my bed."

"Stay just a little while longer, Arduino. It's been so long since I've talked to anyone."

"If you never talk to anyone, how have you managed to keep your voice?" I asked.

"Thanks to the poetry that I remember from my studies, especially the work of Dante. As a student, I memorized many of the verses from his *Commedia*. In the past fourteen months, I have repeated them countless times, savoring their sound, thinking about the meaning of the words, and meditating on their theme . . ."

I was mesmerized by his words, his story.

The Maestro's hoarse cough in the distance startled us both.

"I have to go," I said, panicked. "If he finds me up here, who knows what he'll do."

"Will you visit me again?"

I hesitated. I couldn't think about anything except getting downstairs.

"Well . . ." His sad gaze helped me decide. "Yes, I will come back—as soon as I can."

Chapter Five

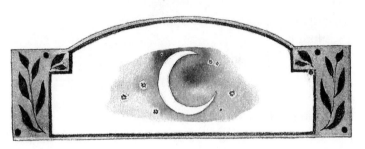

"You blasted boys! The Devil take you! Don't you simpletons know that work doesn't do itself?"

Melania's yelling roused me from my half-sleep. After meeting Donato, I had spent the rest of the night tossing and turning on my pallet under the stairs.

Daylight chased the ghosts from my imagination, but throughout the morning, I could hardly concentrate on my chores.

What should I do? I had discovered a crime. It wasn't legal to keep someone locked up in an attic against his will. My obligation was to denounce the Maestro to the authorities, but the man terrified me. And who would believe me, a lowly apprentice?

"What's the matter with you?" Baldo interrupted my thoughts.

"Nothing." I decided to keep my knowledge of Donato a secret.

We sat down together by the kitchen hearth to eat our lunch.

"Nothing?" he repeated, squinting at me.

"Nothing."

"I know," he said; "you're sick of work."

I nodded. It *was* true. I was tired of cleaning. Who wouldn't be? Besides, if I told him that he was right, he might stop asking me prying questions.

"Yes, I'm tired of it," I said. "The Maestro only lets me touch the brushes if he wants me to clean them. He hasn't asked me to sketch, or even trace a line, since the day I arrived. I feel like a servant."

"Well, you've got a long way to go. I've been here almost a year and the Maestro only lets me watch him draw. He never lets me try it for myself."

He stared into the fire and shook his head as if to chase away evil thoughts. "The truth is," he continued, "I don't care. Painting, ugh! It bores me." His tone was scornful.

"You don't like painting?" I asked, incredulous. "Then what are you doing here?"

He moved back and forth on his ample backside and whispered, "They're making me learn. I told you, my grandfather is Antonio Ferruccio. My family wants me to carry on his art and his . . . business. Either I learn with Cosimo, or I learn with him."

He paused for a moment before continuing in a more serious tone, "My grandfather is a greedy tyrant. He doesn't let me do anything he hasn't ordered me to do. He gives me barely enough food to stay alive—and he uses a whip with more skill than he does a paintbrush. The Maestro doesn't teach me much, and he works me hard, but he doesn't beat me. And the food isn't good, but it's enough —I even manage to get extras now and then. If I could, though, what I'd really like is to learn to cook. My dream is to be the chef in a rich man's house—a house with full pantries."

I could only shake my head. The sons of tailors want to be painters, and the sons of painters, chefs. I wondered what the sons of chefs would want to be!

I spent the next few days in the studio sanding down boards and preparing them with a mixture of plaster of Paris, glue, and water that Piero had made up. It filled the house with a strangely purifying aroma. I hadn't been up to see Donato since my first visit. I didn't want to take any chances.

"Spread it carefully!" barked the Maestro. "Make it perfectly smooth, or the brushstrokes will show!"

Lately, it seemed the Maestro spent most of his time in the studio sitting with a warm woolen compress on his stomach. From time to time, he would yell for Melania to come and change it, which she did with no few complaints.

My thoughts kept turning to Donato. Although I had never liked the Maestro, now that I knew about Donato, his presence was almost more than I could bear. I was filled with the desire to take the pestle I used to grind pigments and beat him with it. But when he looked at me, my thoughts froze.

In my frustration, I began to doubt. What do I care about Donato? I asked myself as I covered the boards with the plaster-of-Paris mixture. I don't really know the boy in the attic; he's not related to me, and he's not my friend. I shouldn't put my future at risk. Painting is more important to me than anything.

But I knew deep down what was right. It was a crime to kidnap someone and keep him prisoner; no man can own another. It was a crime. But what could I do?

At the end of the day, Melania came into the studio to assign our evening chores. "Piero, go and get firewood," she shouted. "Arduino, you fetch the water. Baldo, go around and close all of the shutters. We're going to have a hard frost tonight. When you're done, your supper will be ready."

Frost had already covered the cobbles of the courtyard, and the rope that held the bucket in the well was stiff. Both Piero and Baldo had finished their chores before me and were seated at the kitchen hearth when I returned from the well. Piero had kindly moved my bowl close to the fire, to keep it warm.

". . . But when he opened the door, my poor uncle found a demon with a toad's face and the Devil's horns. He pushed my uncle into the paddock, and with a cord made of dried, braided snakes he . . ."

As they did nearly every night at dinnertime, Melania's

horrible stories held us in rapt attention, and we forgot about the thin, rancid soup we ate and the sweetly sticky odor of the lamp oil. When we had finished eating, and she had finished her tale, we cleaned up and went off to bed.

Late that night, after everyone, including Melania, was fast asleep, I left my tiny corner and listened to the sounds of the household: the Maestro's snores, the last logs in the kitchen hearth falling to embers, the elm branch that scratched the tall studio window, the creaking of the beams —nothing out of the ordinary.

I climbed the stairs to the attic, sat down next to the barred window, lifted the tapestry, and looked in. Light from the full moon flooded the tiny room. Donato, seated on the floor and wrapped in his blanket, was eating.

"Donato," I whispered.

He raised his head and looked at me. I hadn't seen him in several days, and his gaze seemed even calmer to me than before. Perhaps I was the one who was calmer.

"Arduino, thank you for coming back."

"What are you eating?" I asked.

"Well"—he looked into the bowl he held between his hands—"it looks like a soup or gruel. I'm not really sure."

"It's probably the leftover soup that we had for dinner. It was made with something greasy that tasted rancid and stuck in my throat."

"Probably lard," Donato said in his soft voice. "It tastes very good to me."

I thought about this and realized that everything is relative. Things that made me sick to my stomach tasted good to Donato, because he had even less than I.

"Isn't there any way to take off that shackle?" I asked.

"No, the chain links are heavily soldered," Donato explained. "Believe me, in the beginning, I tried everything. Besides, even if I could get the chain off, the door is locked and the windows are all barred."

"And what about Melania? Have you ever asked her for help?"

"I have, and sometimes she looks at me with sympathy —when she looks at me at all. She comes in every night with food, and changes my pail, but usually it's without a word. She's too scared of the Maestro ever to go against him. Without Cosimo, Melania would have nothing, not even a place to sleep. I am grateful to her, though. Without her, I surely would have frozen or starved to death up here."

I had a bitter taste in my mouth. Listening to Donato, I realized what true cowardice was. Was I afraid to help him, for fear of losing my apprenticeship and my chance to become a painter?

"I could tell someone what the Maestro is doing to you," I said. "Turn him in to the authorities, or send for my father, but . . ."

Donato watched me in silence.

"But I . . . I . . ."

My voice choked. At that moment, all of my self-doubt and the difficulty of the situation overwhelmed me.

"Come now, Arduino, what's the matter with you? Are you crying for me?"

"No, no, it's just that I really am such a coward."

"Arduino . . ."

"Yes, I am, and selfish, too," I said without taking a breath. "I could get your freedom tomorrow, but the Maestro would throw me out of the studio, and my father would force me to return to tailoring. As pathetic as it is, this is my only chance to learn to be a painter."

Donato pulled on the chain so that he could get closer to the window.

"Arduino, calm down a minute and listen to me. I don't expect you to sacrifice your dreams for me, nor do I want you to. I know that someday I will be free of this prison. Just knowing that you are my friend gives me some strength. Besides, true freedom isn't in the street, or in Cosimo's studio, or in the air or in the sea. Freedom is inside each one of us."

"But . . ."

"Think about it, Arduino. You aren't really free, either. You have to obey the Maestro and Melania and your father. They occupy your thoughts and perhaps even keep you from living your dreams. I can't move, but my time and thoughts are mine alone. Do you see? I'm freer than you in many ways."

He was right; I was always at the mercy of someone else.

"Don't worry about me," he continued. "You will help me when you're ready. I've survived this long, and I am at peace with myself and others. I would venture to say that I'm even happy, in my own way. Look." He pointed to the floor in a corner of the attic. From where I was, I could make out some marks in the dust. "I can even draw and study perspective, symmetry, and composition."

"You know so much about art," I said. "So much more than I do . . . things I've never even heard of."

"Would you like to learn some of them?"

"Yes, but how?"

"Come up here when you can. I'll teach you what I can."

I looked at him. In spite of his uncombed hair and his dirty, threadbare velvet doublet, he was an elegant man. I thought I recognized my grandfather's wisdom in his young eyes.

"Yes, Donato," I said. "I will come up—every chance I get."

Chapter Six

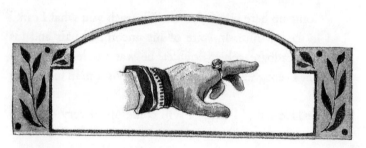

The weeks that followed were the most intense that I can remember. During the day, I helped Melania clean and organize the house; I worked in the studio and took care of the horse. At night, I crept up the attic stairs to meet with Donato. We were careful to whisper and make as little noise as possible, so as not to wake anyone sleeping below. I had taken some supplies from the studio—a pencil, some paper, a brush, and some paints—which Donato stored in the attic. By the light of the moon—when there was one—he showed me everything that he had learned from the Maestro, as well as what he'd discovered within the walls of his prison, about light, shadow, reflections, lines, and angles.

In the mornings, I dragged through my chores, but despite my exhaustion, I was energized by my friendship with

Donato and by everything he was teaching me. My father had sent me a letter at Christmastime saying that everyone at home was well and thinking of me, as well as a package with new clothes and some roasted chestnuts. I took the chestnuts up to the attic, where Donato and I celebrated the holiday on our own.

For the first time since I'd arrived at the studio, I felt happy, though my happiness was always tempered by worry for Donato and a feeling of helplessness. But it wouldn't be long before something would happen to change the course of all our lives . . .

"Boy!" Melania yelled. She was in top form that morning. "Are you in love with the broom? You're asleep with her in your arms!"

Baldo and Piero laughed, and Marco looked me over from top to bottom, sneering.

"What's going on out there?" the Maestro thundered from the depths of his bedchamber.

"Nothing's going on!" Melania shot back. Then in a voice only we could hear, she added, "Drooling magpie! If you want to know what's going on, get out of bed and come see!"

He finally entered the studio that day after lunch. This was late, even for him.

Baldo and I were preparing an egg-yolk-and-vinegar adhesive, while Piero and Marco worked on their projects, when we all heard three loud knocks at the front door.

Baldo and I looked at each other. Who could it be? Since

I'd been there, Cosimo di Forlì's house had had only two regular visitors: the cold and the local priest, and the priest came only in the mornings.

"Melania! See who it is!" bellowed the Maestro from his seat by the fire.

"Yes, yes, I'm going," she called from the kitchen.

A moment later, she was at the studio door.

"There's a nobleman outside!" she said, excitedly.

"What did you say? Who is it?" growled Cosimo.

"A nobleman, with a lot of servants!"

I'd never seen Melania so nervous. The Maestro stood up and, with Melania's help, slowly dragged his hunched figure down the hall. When they both disappeared behind the curtain that separated the entryway from the hallway, the four of us boys crept quietly after them and peered as best we could through a narrow opening in the curtain.

The Maestro looked through the peephole and then closed it with a bang. He straightened up, pushed back his hair with his hands, smoothed his robe, and opened the heavy door.

There stood the noble Duke of Algora. I recognized him immediately: he was one of my father's best clients. I also recognized his woolen cloak—my father's work.

"Greetings, Maestro," said the Duke in a dignified tone. "How do you do?"

"Very well, my lord," said Cosimo. "But come in, come in, please. It is much too cold outside."

The Duke made a small signal with his hand and two of his servants helped him remove his cloak.

He entered the room slowly, looking around impassively, as was to be expected of someone of his class. The thin, red-clad form of his secretary slid in behind him. The other men in his entourage stayed in the street, by the luxurious coach in which the Duke had arrived.

The Maestro closed the door and offered the Duke one of the chairs at the table in the entryway. Then he sat down and ordered Melania to fetch an oil lamp. We jumped back from the curtain as she brushed past us. She was so nervous she forgot to order us all back to the studio. We resumed our positions at the curtain.

"Dear Maestro," began the nobleman, "I would like to know if there is time in your schedule to undertake a new project. If so, I have a commission for you."

The Maestro leaned on the edge of the table in order to stand up again. Melania glared at us before she entered the room with the lamp, which she set down next to the Duke.

"My lord, I'm honored that you would come to me," said the Maestro.

The Duke smiled and removed his gloves.

"How could I go elsewhere? Your marvelous allegory on freedom graces all the festivities in my grand ballroom."

Allegory on freedom! Cosimo had painted an allegory on freedom! Cosimo di Forlì, who kept his best student prisoner for being a better artist than he was! I felt my mouth fill with bile. This was my Maestro, a man from whom I could learn only hypocrisy.

"My daughter is marrying, dear Maestro," the Duke continued.

"Little Bianca," said Cosimo, with a wide smile.

"Not so little anymore." He laughed. "She's nearly fifteen years old."

"She's a lovely creature," the Maestro gushed.

"Yes, she's very lovely. But the palace chapel is a bit, how shall I say, a bit unlovely, yes, that's the word. My lady and I thought that if the wall behind the altar were painted, it would be much more attractive."

"But of course. My lady the Duchess has exquisite taste —all of Florence is of that opinion."

How would the Maestro know what all of Florence thinks when he never leaves his dirty old house, I wondered. It was all false praise.

"We hope that you, Maestro di Forlì, will prepare a sketch of your ideas for the chapel wall painting."

"It will be a pleasure, my lord. I will draw and deliver it myself."

The nobleman rose from his chair. He stretched his hand to his secretary, who handed him a small pouch. It jingled with coins.

"Forty ducats for your initial expenses," said the Duke, placing the pouch on the table. "When you present the sketch, if it is to our liking, you will receive another such payment. We will then determine the balance of your fee, for the actual painting, which will depend on the materials you need and the amount of work necessary to prepare the wall. Are you in agreement?"

Cosimo put his hand on the pouch. "Thank you, my lord. You are always so generous. Both you and your distinguished wife will be satisfied. It will be my master-piece, I can assure you. But one thing . . ."

"Yes?"

"The theme, my lord. What do you wish the painting to represent?"

"That is up to your imagination, my dear Maestro. You are the artist."

The Duke and his secretary moved toward the door, which the Maestro opened for them. Just outside, the Duke put on his cloak, with the help of two servants.

"The wedding is to be in early summer," he said. "I hope you will remember that your time is limited, Maestro."

"Of course, of course. Do not worry, my lord."

Cosimo closed the door, turned around, and pressed his hands to his stomach. From his expression, he seemed to be in great pain.

"Melania!" he howled.

"God save me!" exclaimed the servant.

"Build up the fire; it's freezing in this house. And make me some broth and hot wine!"

We hurried back to the studio.

"What's wrong with him?" I asked Piero.

"Nothing," answered Piero in a thin voice. "He has a commission."

"Arduino!" The Maestro's shout made my hair stand on end.

"Yes, Maestro."

"Sharpen all the charcoals. Clean the brushes and the

palettes; I want everything as good as new. Do you understand?"

"Yes, Maestro."

And from that moment on, the whole house was in a frenzy. Melania worked in the kitchen and kept after us with a vengeance. I did whatever I was told, while Piero prepared the materials that would be used for the first sketch. Baldo cleaned the tables before putting down new sheets of paper. He took advantage of the confusion to go in and out of the kitchen, eating what he could find. Marco went through an enormous portfolio of drawings, separating the religious themes from the mythological and ornamental ones. The Maestro had announced that the theme of the fresco would be the marriage of the Virgin.

That night, I sat next to the barred window and described to Donato, in detail, everything that had happened that day.

"I wonder if he can handle this commission," I said.

"Why wouldn't he? He's done it many times before."

"But he gets so nervous," I explained. "Besides, I think he's ill."

"Ill?"

"Yes, I told you he'd been acting strangely these last few weeks—getting up late, the hot compresses, and all that. Today, he could barely walk to the front door without Melania's help."

Donato was silent; then he sighed and rubbed his eyes.

"This will be your opportunity, Arduino. The painting

in the Duke's chapel will be a fresco—a very complicated undertaking. Cosimo will need all the help he can get; I'm sure he'll have something for you to do."

"Of course he will—I'll get to break the eggs to make the base."

Donato covered his mouth to stifle a laugh. "Let me tell you about fresco painting . . ."

That night I began to learn the best way to prepare the walls and the way to trace the drawings with perforated paper; how to plan the work according to colors; how to shade with the color still partially wet; and how to keep the color from running.

We talked all night, until a half-dozen chirping sparrows signaled the onset of a new day. Only then did I make my way back down to my pallet, so Melania wouldn't miss me when she woke up.

Chapter Seven

During the days that followed, the Maestro worked on several sketches. He drew on large, fresh sheets of paper, which several times, in frustration, he ripped up, only to begin again. Marco helped him, while Piero, Baldo, and I tidied the studio, prepared paper, and furtively looked over Maestro's shoulder every time we passed behind him.

He worked feverishly and stopped only to drink the cups of tea and broth that Melania brought to him, or when he doubled up with a groan, clutching his belly.

One night, when Donato and I were discussing the effect of backlighting on an interior scene, I heard the Maestro's violent cough from a distant corner of the house. I looked down toward the kitchen and saw Melania's candle. My temples began to pound.

"Something's wrong!" I whispered. "I have to go."

I flew down the stairs without saying goodbye to Donato and threw myself headfirst onto my pallet, certain that my visits to the attic had been discovered. I was lying there panting when Melania called to me in a frightened voice.

"Arduino, wake up, boy! The Maestro is very ill."

I got up and followed her, relieved that my secret was still safe. But why was she calling me to help her? What could I do?

We went across the hall and entered the Maestro's bed-chamber. I shivered. In all the months that I had lived in his house, I had never been in his room.

I looked around. There was a tall four-poster bed with a canopy, a trunk with rusted rings and hinges, and a chair with a grimy leather seat.

"Melania," Maestro called out in an anguished voice.

"Yes, yes, I'm here."

"Melania," he repeated.

Slowly, I moved closer to the bed. The Maestro's pale face was surrounded by cobwebs of gray hair. His forehead was beaded with sweat.

"Here," Melania said brusquely. She held a rusty pan toward me.

I took it, but I didn't act quickly enough. The Maestro suddenly sat up, threw his head forward, and vomited.

I felt the room spin around me. I was overwhelmed by nausea.

"Hold the pan steady!" Melania yelled. "Can't you see that he's making a mess everywhere?"

"What do you want me to do?"

"What do you think I want you to do? Make sure he vomits in the pan."

It wasn't easy. The Maestro moved from side to side in his bed, and I could hardly breathe, much less watch what I was doing. Although only minutes had passed, it seemed that I had spent my whole life next to that bed.

Melania stripped the soiled blanket from the bed and took the pan from my hands. The Maestro was covered only by a thin sheet.

"Arduino, you must go for the doctor," she said.

"The doctor? Why me? I don't know where he lives, and besides, I'm all wet and dirty," I protested. I thought of all her stories of the dangerous criminals who wandered the streets.

"Come with me," she said, and we headed back to the kitchen. She set the pan on the floor, then took a rag from a hook near the hearth and began to wipe me off.

"You'll have time to wash later," she said, then lowered her voice. "The Maestro is very ill. The doctor has got to see him. I'll tell you how to find his house."

"What about the other boys?" I asked. "Marco is the oldest. Make him go."

"Marco won't go, and he doesn't have to. He has a special contract," she said as we walked down the corridor. "Piero is so delicate that I don't dare send him anywhere, and Baldo . . . well, Baldo never does anything right."

"But I—"

"You are the most intelligent and the most sensible," Melania said, resting her heavy hand on my shoulder.

I didn't say anything more, feeling both fear and pride.

"Go outside and turn right. Keep going until you get to a square with a statue of Saint Francis. There you'll see three streets; take the one on the far left, the narrowest one. The doctor lives in the second house on the right. You'll recognize his door easily, because the knocker is in the shape of a fleur-de-lis."

"But—"

"Ask for the doctor. His name is Mitone. Tell him that the Maestro is very ill. He'll come running. They're good friends."

"But I—I can't," I stammered. I was sure I was going to be a victim of some vicious murderer.

Melania pushed me into the street and yelled, "Go on, run! Can't you see that the Maestro is dying! Now hurry!"

The door slammed behind me.

Outside, the frigid air relieved the bitter smell of my clothes and cleared my head. I had to try to forget my crazy fears.

I've got to get the doctor, I thought. If the Maestro dies . . .

As soon as I thought it, I felt rotten and selfish again. Did I care about the Maestro's health only in terms of how it would affect my future? This could be my chance to help Donato. But what if the Maestro did die because I hadn't brought the doctor? As despicable as he was, I would have to live with that knowledge for the rest of my life. It was a choice between one man's imprisonment and another man's death! Tonight, I would have to follow Melania's instructions.

As I made my way down the street, I felt along the wall for a sense of security, touching rough stones, bricks, wooden doors, and moldy bellpulls.

The thought of encountering a criminal kept me on edge.

A cat jumped from a windowsill as I passed. I stopped and listened so closely to every sound that I thought my head would jump from my shoulders. I continued on.

"I am the son of Emilio Neri, and I will be a Florentine artist," I said to myself. Repeating those words gave me a sense of courage as I made my way into the night.

When the wall ended, I had reached a corner, but the square was dark and I couldn't see any statue.

I hesitated and looked around. To my left, I saw a tiny ray of light that shone out of a shutter; it was far away, at the end of a street.

I hoped it was the street on the left that Melania told me to look for; I couldn't see whether there were two other streets to the right of it. At that moment, I felt the safest thing was to go toward the light. I left the wall and crossed the square slowly so I wouldn't trip. Just before I reached the other side, I heard a splash and felt cold water fill my shoe. I had stepped in a puddle. The cold water felt as though it would cut through my leg.

I stumbled the rest of the way across the square and leaned against a wall to empty my shoe. Why should I have to put up with this? I thought with anger. My father pays good money for the Maestro to teach me to paint, not for me to sleep on the floor, and eat terrible food, and go out in the middle of the night, frozen and dirty . . .

At least my tears were hot. I thought of running away; I would go as far away as I could and live the way I wanted, on my own, or even at sea with pirates . . . Anything would be better than this nightmare.

A clock somewhere struck one. I started down the street, still touching the walls as I went along. I paid close attention to the door knockers as I passed each building; I didn't want to pass the doctor's house.

One door . . . two windows . . . an empty niche, and finally another door. Anxiously, I peered at the knocker. It was in shape of the fleur-de-lis, which I had drawn so many times before. Never had it seemed so lovely to me.

I knocked four times, but no answer. I figured the household was asleep, and tried again. This time it worked.

"I'm coming, I'm coming." It was a woman's voice.

The top half of the door opened, and a very sleepy face, topped with a red woolen nightcap, peered out at me.

"What do you want?" Her tone was understandably gruff.

"My Maestro is very ill. He needs Dr. Mitone," I answered.

"Who is your Maestro?"

"Cosimo di Forlì."

"Wait here," said the woman, and she shut the door.

Before long, the door opened again and a tall, thin man wrapped in a long cloak stepped out.

"What's wrong with Cosimo?" he asked.

"I don't know, sir. He's been vomiting . . . his stomach hurts . . . he coughs a lot . . ."

The doctor went back inside to get a lantern. When he returned, we started back toward the Maestro's house. We walked in silence, though the doctor kept a brisk pace which, despite my frozen feet, I managed to keep up with.

As we passed through the square, by the light of the lantern I could see the statue of Saint Francis that I had missed on my way there.

Finally, we reached the house. The doctor knocked firmly on the door. It creaked open in the cold, and Melania let us in, talking all the while.

"Thank you so much for coming, Doctor. The Maestro has been ill for some time, but he refuses to take care of himself . . . I've wanted to call for you many times, but he's never let me. You know he's as stubborn as a mule . . ."

They went into the bedroom and I stayed in the kitchen, by the fire that Melania had stirred up from the embers. I stared into the flames. I was stiff from the cold. I wasn't sure how long I stood there, but Melania's voice interrupted my thoughts.

"What are you doing so close to the fire? Are you trying to burn the house down? That's just what we need!"

I looked at her. She was red and out of breath.

"Where is the doctor?" I asked.

"He left a few minutes ago."

How long had I been standing there? "What's wrong with the Maestro?"

"Well, Dr. Mitone says the Maestro's stomach is blocked and half-rotten. He'll have to stay in bed and eat lots of vegetables for a while."

As she looked at me, her expression became sweeter.

"You poor boy, you're wet and dirty. Wait just a moment."

Melania put a pot of water on the stove and then went into the laundry. She emerged with a large wooden tub and a block of soap. She filled the tub partway with cold water, then we sat together at the kitchen table, waiting for the pot of water to boil. When it did, she poured it into the tub, filling it a few more inches. Then she cut off a small slab of soap from the block and handed it to me.

"Come on, take off those dirty rags and get in. I'll get you some clean clothes."

The warm bath was delicious. I had gone out into the night, done what I was supposed to do, and returned safely. For me, that was the real triumph, and a bath was my reward.

A little while later, Melania returned with clean clothes for me.

"You've been a good lad. I knew I could count on you. I have had a lot of experience with boys. You are one of the good ones. You deserve a better life than this nest of misery and envy."

She sighed as she combed out my hair. "If I could choose . . . It's hard to be born a woman and a servant. Always obeying, even when the person who gives you orders is mean and miserable. Always silent, even when you don't agree. Bearing everything, everything."

Melania had never talked like this to me, and I was moved by her words. But before I could say anything, the Maestro's anguished voice rang out from his room, and Melania was away down the hall again.

Chapter Eight

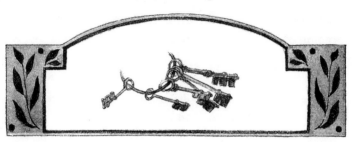

The Maestro continued sketching from his bed, but his hands were shaky, and his vision betrayed the lines that he saw in his mind's eye. Day after day, his condition got worse. Even his yelling grew weaker.

One morning, after working for hours—with everyone coming and going between the studio and the bedroom with paper, pencils, easel, and supports—the Maestro gave up on the drawing. Marco and I witnessed it from his bedside.

"It's impossible, impossible . . . I'll never finish it," he said. "The Duke will be so disappointed in me! My God, commissions like this one are few and far between, and now . . . now . . ." His voice came to a choking halt, and he leaned back on his pillows.

I looked at his sketch. Most of it was a mess. There were only two partially completed figures. The Maestro had barely begun!

"Maestro, Maestro," whispered Marco.

I ran back to the studio to tell the other boys.

"If there's no work and the Maestro can't teach, what will become of us?" asked Baldo, nibbling the heel of a loaf of bread.

"It's not just the money," explained Piero. "It's a loss of prestige, too. A well-executed commission brings in more commissions. It's like a chain."

Baldo stopped eating. "I'll tell you what I think will become of us. Our lives will be ruined. If we don't finish our apprenticeships, the time we've spent here won't count for anything. We'll all have to start over. Well, I'll run away first, before anyone can force me to return home."

Baldo's words of doom had a silencing effect on us. Even if he was exaggerating, there was some truth to what he said.

Later, when I went into the bedroom with new candles, Marco was there trying to finish the drawing, to the Maestro's impatient instructions.

"Make that form a little rounder. The curve of the head should harmonize with the lines of the back and the legs . . . No . . . No! Not like that! You don't understand anything, Marco. I don't know what I'm going to do with you. You've been here for so long, yet every day it seems you know less."

"Maestro, I'm doing my best," Marco said in a quavering voice.

"If you're not even capable of doing the sketch according to my instructions, how are you going to do the fresco? It's impossible, impossible. It would be better for me to send a message to the Duke right now so that he can give the commission to another painter. My God! I can't believe it's come to that! Cosimo di Forlì, turning down a commission!"

Marco fell to his knees next to the bed and buried his face in the covers. He began crying and hiccuping.

As I stood in the doorway, I got up my nerve to say something. "Why don't you hire a specialist?"

"A specialist!" howled the Maestro. "A specialist in what, every aspect of painting? It wouldn't be my studio's work then; it would be a stranger's work. It wouldn't even have my style or my color. No, I'd rather give up the commission rather than try to make this shameful mess any better."

And with a quick movement, he pulled the covers up to his chin, then turned to face the wall.

Marco jumped up and ran out. For some minutes, the only sound was the sputtering of the candles, and, off in the distance, Marco's sobbing.

I was still standing in the doorway. Suddenly I had an idea that made my head spin and at the same time seemed extraordinarily perfect. It could be the solution to the Maestro's desperate situation, which affected us all, but, most important, it might be the one way I could really help

Donato. The only problem was how to put my idea into words.

"Maestro," I said, quietly.

A little groan came from the blankets.

"I think I have an idea that . . . could . . . could save the commission."

The candle flames seemed to dance before my eyes.

"What is it?" he said gruffly, still facing the wall.

"Donato." I whispered his name.

Cosimo sat straight up in bed.

"What did you say? Where did you hear that name?"

His face drained of its color, with an expression so fierce that I felt that the house, Florence, and the whole world were about to fall on my head. I kept silent, not sure of the best way to answer his question.

"Well, answer me! How do you know about Donato?"

"I . . . Maestro . . ." My voice faltered.

"How could you? How could you know about Donato? Melania! Melania!" He began to get out of bed.

The servant came running.

"What's going on here?" she bellowed. "Why in the world are you calling me like that? Mother of mercy!" she shouted when she saw the Maestro. "Get back in bed! Do you want to lose your insides right here?"

"Arduino . . . How does he know about Donato? What have you told him?"

Melania pushed the patient back into his bed and covered him up. She sat in the leather chair and spoke in a firm voice. "Now tell me. What is going on?"

The Maestro didn't answer. He moved his head from side to side, groaning.

"He's angry with me because I told him that Donato could help him finish the Duke's commission," I said, without pausing for breath.

Melania looked stunned. Then the expression in her eyes seemed to change to one of hope.

"Do you really think that Donato could do it?"

"I'm sure of it," I answered.

"Even after so much time without painting?"

I nodded.

Melania moved closer to the bed.

"Maestro, listen to me. The boy's idea is a good one."

"But how did he know about Donato?" Cosimo repeated.

"That makes no difference. You know what's important now . . ."

To set Donato free, I thought. From the look on Melania's face, I had a feeling that she thought the same thing.

For a few minutes, everyone was silent. The Maestro closed his eyes. Melania and I waited. Sweat beaded my brow.

Finally the Maestro opened his eyes and spoke. His voice was weak.

"He won't want to do it. He'll only want to kill me."

Melania turned to me. "What do you think?"

"He'll do it," I said.

The Maestro sat up in bed and stared into my eyes with his yellowish gaze. "You can't be sure, can you?"

I didn't answer, but kept looking at him.

"Come now, Maestro," Melania said. "You have no other choice."

Cosimo lay back down and turned his head away from us.

"Give him the keys," he said.

Melania pulled a cord out from the folds of her skirt and untied the large key at the end of it.

"This is the key to the attic door." She handed it to me.

Then she went to the trunk and took out a wooden box, which held a smaller key: the one to Donato's shackle.

The keys! Without wasting another second, I turned and ran to the stairs.

I talked in a rush, telling Donato everything that had happened, as I fought with the rusty lock on the attic door. Donato listened quietly from the other side. When I finally pushed the door open, he crawled over to me, took my hand, and kissed it. The gesture embarrassed me. He was my true Maestro, and here he was kissing my hand, thanking me. I knelt down and hugged him. He felt frail, like a child in my arms. Though we were both overwhelmed with emotion, neither of us said a word.

I pulled away and took out the key to the shackle. Finally freed, Donato stood up, brushed his tattered clothes, and embraced me again.

"I knew you would help me, Arduino. I knew you would find a way."

Together we walked out the door and down the stairs. Donato's legs were weak from inactivity, so he leaned on my arm to steady himself. With his other hand he held tightly to the rope banister.

We slowly made our way to the bedroom, then stopped just outside the door.

Donato wiped his brow, raised his chin, and walked in, alone. Melania moved aside as he approached the bed.

"Donato," whispered the Maestro, in a trembling voice.

Donato seemed to be taking in the Maestro's appearance: his gray hair, his tired eyes, surrounded with wrinkles of worry, and his pale, crumpled mouth.

"Maestro," he said in a strange voice.

"Donato," Cosimo repeated. "I have been . . . unjust with you. I didn't want . . . I was afraid . . . and I let my jealousy get the better of me. Your art blinded me. I . . . God forgive me."

Donato sighed deeply, rubbed his hands, and said, "Give me something to eat, and a bath, and I will begin."

"But . . ." the Maestro began confusedly.

"Where is the sketch?"

"Arduino will show it to you," the Maestro said, allowing some hope to creep into his voice. Melania had already left the room to fetch some food, and to prepare the bath.

Donato soaked in the tub for nearly an hour. After he dressed and ate, we headed into the studio. Donato seemed to be walking on clouds. He looked around the room, his eyes shining. Every detail, even as small as the nicked corner of a table, seemed to fill him with emotion.

"Maestro," I said as I came up to him, "here is the sketch." I pointed toward it.

"Maestro," Donato repeated. He ignored where I had pointed, but looked into my eyes with an indefinable expression. Then he smiled. It was joy.

Just then Marco, who had been sitting on his stool with his face buried in his hands, lifted his head and looked at Donato with shock.

"You?"

"Good afternoon, Marco," said Donato merrily.

The color drained from Marco's face.

"Donato, where have you been? What are you doing here?"

Donato grinned. "Don't worry. I'm nothing more than a ghost."

Marco let out a shrill scream, and then ran out into the hallway.

"Only a ghost," Donato said to himself.

"He's still a genius," Donato said when he saw the Maestro's sketch.

"What?" I said. I couldn't believe Donato was impressed with the Maestro's meager efforts.

"Cosimo still has his talent," he said. "His bad temper, bitterness, and avarice haven't managed to kill his art. The only thing that doesn't fit are these lines . . . they seem less inspired, clumsy, even."

"Marco drew that part," I explained, amazed at how he immediately saw the distinction.

"Poor Marco," he commented, lowering his voice. "He'll never be a good painter."

"He works hard, though," I said. "And Cosimo teaches him more than he does everyone else."

Donato took one of the charcoals that I had prepared for him, and rolled it between his fingers.

"Marco is a very proud boy. Once, during a rare friendly moment, he told me a little about himself. He said his family has more distinguished ancestors than money, though they have plenty of that, too. They wanted Marco to be a military officer, but he refused. The priesthood or painting were his only other options. He chose painting even though he doesn't have a real talent or passion for it. His family pays Cosimo quite a lot to keep him on."

"I wonder what he would really like to do."

Donato shrugged. "Who knows? Maybe he'd like to watch the time pass between the strings of his lute."

I kept silent. Donato was drawing, and all the problems, miseries, and fears that had weighed me down disappeared as I watched him work. His clearly drawn lines, soft shadows, and crisp contrasts were magical.

After working for hours, Donato finally stood up from the work table. He sighed and straightened his shirt.

"Do you remember what I told you, Arduino?" he said. "You must see the work as a whole, yet evaluate the intensity of each of the elements in the picture . . ."

He backed up a few paces and bumped into Baldo and Piero, who had been looking over his shoulder, open-mouthed. Baldo sat down on the floor with a smack. We looked at one another without knowing what to say, and suddenly all four of us burst out laughing. It was the best introduction possible between my new Maestro and my companions.

Chapter Nine

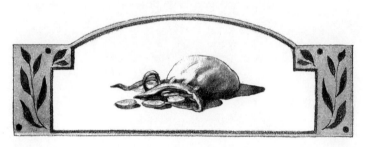

The Maestro silently contemplated the finished sketch that Donato held out in front of him. A few tears slid from his eyes, though whether they were tears of emotion or simply caused by the effort of looking was not clear. Finally, with a trembling gesture, he sighed and said, "This work is worthy of my studio."

Donato looked at me with satisfaction.

"You must take it to the Duke's palace," the Maestro continued in an exhausted voice. "I told him I would deliver it, but then he'd realize how ill I am, and that would lead him to doubt that I can carry out the commission. The word would spread, and I'd soon be out of work. He must not know that I am ill, nor must he know that the art is not my own."

"He won't find out," said Donato, looking down. I knew that he was reluctant to lie to the Duke, but it seemed the only choice.

"Melania!" croaked the Maestro. "Where does that woman get to?"

The servant arrived, shaking flour from her wrinkled woolen skirt.

"Whether ill or well, the man does nothing but insult and interrupt me," she growled. "Curses!"

"Stop moaning and listen. Have the boys hitch the horse to the cart and wrap this sketch in cloth."

Melania looked at the drawing that Donato and I held against the bed.

"You are a true artist, Donato," she said softly.

"Come along, come along," barked the Maestro. "You're wasting time."

Before Melania could disappear down the hallway, he added, "And get some clean clothes out for Donato and Marco. They must make a good impression."

"I'm taking Arduino with me." Donato's steady voice surprised me. He wanted me for his assistant! Though I was his friend, I was still the newest and the least experienced.

"Marco should be the one to go with you. He's the one that knows—" began Cosimo.

"I'm taking Arduino with me," Donato repeated.

Cosimo shrugged his shoulders and buried himself in his pillows and covers. Donato signaled to me, and we left the room, carrying the large sketch between us.

"Pay my respects to the Duke," said the Maestro from under his blankets.

The brilliant marble entrance hall in the Duke's palace was flooded with light. We sat waiting on a soft blue velvet bench. Donato, who was dressed in black and seemed even thinner and paler because of it, was examining the perfectly proportioned arches that circled the room. The vastness of the hall made me feel as insecure as a chick out of its nest. At the same time, I was thrilled to be exactly where I was.

A boy wearing tight-fitting hose entered the room and announced the Duke, who strode in behind him. He was wearing a fur-lined robe. This one I didn't recognize as my father's work.

"Well?" he asked in an indifferent tone.

Donato spoke. "My Maestro, Cosimo di Forlì, sends you his respects, sir. On his behalf we are here to present you with a sketch, which you were good enough to commission him to create."

The Duke looked at Donato with interest now.

"Where is the Maestro?" he asked, surprised.

"My Maestro is old, and the winter has been a hard one, my lord. Pray forgive us, and accept us as his ambassadors."

"Show me the sketch."

We uncovered the drawing and placed it in the light. The Duke looked at it for some time.

"It's brilliant," he said, "just as are all the works of Cosimo di Forlì's hand." He looked up at Donato. "Tell

your Maestro that I am most eager to see my chapel deco-
rated in this marvelous theme, so beautifully realized by his
art." He then snapped his fingers, and his secretary, who
must have been standing just outside the door, entered the
room. The Duke spoke to him, and the secretary left. He
returned a moment later with a suede pouch, tied with a
silken cord. The Duke took it and held it for a moment as
if weighing it.

"Give this to the Maestro," he said, handing the bag to
Donato. "These coins are the second part of his payment,
as we agreed."

Donato bowed. "Thank you, my lord."

"What is your name?" asked the Duke curiously.

"Donato, sir."

"And have you been with Cosimo a long time?"

Donato smiled and answered, "An eternity, my lord."

I had never been as happy as I was during the days that
followed, working in the palace chapel. I loved all of the
jobs that I was asked to carry out: climbing the scaffolding,
preparing and smoothing the wall, studying the proportions
of the original drawing and the panel, mixing the colors,
scaling the drawings, tracing, perforating . . . nothing bored
me. Donato had organized the work so that I would partici-
pate in all of the steps. The others helped, too; Marco
listened grudgingly to Donato's instructions, though Baldo
and Piero obeyed the young Maestro's orders without complaining. Baldo's attention was often on the windows,

through which he could see the cartloads of provisions—
sometimes exotic fruits and vegetables—that arrived daily
at the palace.

I was fascinated—and intimidated—by the complicated
technique of fresco painting, but Donato's patient instruction helped increase my confidence.

". . . The plaster must be fresh when the colors are
applied."

Green, violet, azure, we matched all of the colors to the
feathers of the birds that the Duke collected and kept in an
enormous aviary on the palace grounds.

". . . If the plaster is dry, the paint will not take properly
and will fall off in scales . . ."

The fat little terra-cotta cherubs near the altar laughed
silently at the fauns carved on the ends of the pews.

". . . You can't retouch the paint once it has dried, either.
It would look like a patch, and be very obvious."

Each day, just before sundown, we finished up what we
were working on and prepared to return to the studio.
Usually the five of us left at the same time. On one particular afternoon, however, the Duke was coming to the chapel
to check on the progress of the fresco, and Donato was to
stay late.

"Stay with me, Arduino," Donato had said, and I had
agreed. Hearing this, Marco left, slamming the chapel door
behind him. Piero and Baldo had already gone back to the
Maestro's.

While we waited, Donato and I chatted about the next

day's work. Finally the Duke of Algora arrived, along with his daughter Bianca, the betrothed. Again, the Duke asked where the Maestro was, and again Donato made an excuse for him.

Bianca looked like a child, with curly auburn hair braided with pearls. She glanced around with sad blue eyes.

"The Maestro is a good teacher," the Duke commented. "His apprentice here is able to follow his style exactly, though he seems to add something of his own to the work."

Donato looked down, modestly.

"Tell me, Donato, will it be finished in time?"

"Yes, my lord. As you can see, the most complicated part —preparing the full-size drawings—is finished. The painting is proceeding at a regular pace, day by day."

He took the Duke to the table with stacks of drawings, leaving me standing alone with Bianca.

"It will be a beautiful painting," Bianca said in a soft voice. "It must be wonderful to devote your life to art."

"You appreciate art, my lady," I said nervously. "We are very lucky to be working for you."

"Luck was yours at birth," she said pensively.

"I beg your pardon?"

She sat down on a bench, her dress of golden taffeta rustling around her.

"You are a man; you can choose what you like. You can decide your life and your destiny. That is why you are lucky."

"It is not easy to choose or to decide, my lady. One must fight and suffer to reach one's dreams."

"You, at least, can choose."

Her voice was so sad that it seemed night fell more rapidly.

"You are a wealthy young lady," I said, feebly trying to cheer her. "You lack for nothing and are safe from hunger, and cold, and fear. Your life is peaceful."

During some minutes, the only sound in the chapel was that of the sheets of paper Donato was unfolding before the Duke.

"My destiny from the day I was born was marriage and motherhood," she said. "Even the choice of husband was made for me. If I had the chance, I would like to be an artist and work in a studio with a great Maestro like yours, and paint the things that are felt in the heart. I wish I could paint feelings."

"Paint feelings?"

"Yes," she said, smiling. "Joy, pain, boredom, love, anger . . ."

"But . . ."

"But I'm only a woman. I can only obey and dream."

"But—"

"Come along, Bianca," interrupted the Duke. "It's getting late."

The girl stood up, nodded to me, and left the chapel, leaving only the sound of her dainty slippers behind her.

.   .   .

Donato and I returned to the house together. He was in high spirits from the Duke's favorable opinion of his work. I was so absorbed by the memory of my conversation with the Duke's daughter that I didn't notice anything strange until I went to the studio to drop off some drawings. When Marco saw me, he scurried out of the room. Baldo, who was cleaning brushes, looked at me, rolled his eyes, and made a sign—his forefinger moving across his neck.

"What's wrong?" I asked him.

"Arduino!" The Maestro's voice echoed through the whole house.

"Yes, yes," I called back, startled.

"Arduino!" he repeated, and my temples began to pound.

I ran to his room, and stood in front of the bed. He was sitting up, half-dressed, his eyes red with fury.

"Yes, Maestro," I said.

"Maestro?" he yelled. "I'm not your Maestro, and I never will be again. I have had rude, stupid boys in my studio, but you're the worst of all!"

"What have I done?" I asked. I was bewildered by this outburst.

"You have the nerve to ask me? Of course, I had forgotten. You are Arduino di Emilio di Antonio Neri, prince of traitors!"

My legs were shaking, and I would have fallen to the floor if Melania's callused hands hadn't held me up.

"Come along, let's go," she said.

"But what have I done?" I repeated, louder.

No one would answer me. I sat on the kitchen hearth next to the fire, going over everything that had happened during the day, but I couldn't think of anything that would have brought on the Maestro's fit of rage.

"Baldo," I called, when I saw my companion tiptoe by the kitchen. "Baldo!"

"Shhh!" he said. He came in and took some nuts from a basket on the table.

"Baldo, tell me what has happened. I don't understand what's going on."

"I can't tell you."

"Why not?"

Baldo shrugged and tried to crack one of the nuts with his teeth.

"Where's Donato?"

Baldo shrugged again and ran out of the kitchen. Melania came in, looked at me, and shook her head.

"Where's Donato?" I asked her.

"The Maestro sent him on an errand."

"Donato? Why not Marco or Piero?"

Just then I heard the heavy knocker strike the front door. I ran down the hallway, hoping it was Donato. I pulled hard on the handle and the door swung open.

There, on the doorstep, was my father. I was stunned.

He stepped into the house and, without a word, put both his hands on my shoulders and looked into my eyes. His expression gave me a terrible sinking feeling. Piero, who had apparently accompanied him, vanished like smoke behind the curtain.

"Is that you, Maestro Emilio?" shouted the Maestro from his room.

"Yes, it is," my father replied, turning to follow Cosimo's voice to the bedroom. "Come," he said to me, and I quietly walked behind.

As soon as the Maestro saw my father, he started ranting. "You remember the instructions you gave when we formalized the contract for your son's apprenticeship: 'If at any time the boy misbehaves or does not do his work, send for me.' Are they not, more or less, your words?"

"Yes," my father answered.

"Well, that is just what I have done. Your son is the most disgraceful traitor that I have ever known. Take him out of my sight. Melania!"

The servant came into the bedchamber carrying my old satchel, which she laid at my father's feet.

"What has Arduino done?" he asked in a severe voice.

"Ask him yourself."

My father looked at me, and his eyes tore me apart.

"Well, what have you done?" he said angrily.

"Nothing, Father."

"Nothing? What do you mean, nothing? Is this some kind of joke?" His voice boomed, and he turned to the Maestro again. "I demand an explanation immediately."

The Maestro relaxed against the cushions, seeming to enjoy the scene, and explained.

"Your son, Maestro Emilio, betrayed the confidence that I placed in him. Against my specific instructions, he revealed to the Duke of Algora, my client, that I was ill and that the commissioned work in his chapel was not my own." He paused and then went on, ignoring my surprised look. "He's jeopardized not only the commission but the future of this studio. When word gets out, no one will ever come to me again for work. I'll be ruined!"

My father turned to me for an explanation, but I was in shock. All I could say was "It isn't true."

The Maestro swung his legs out from under the blankets and tried to stand. His face was red, and two veins stood out at his temples.

"Do you see? Now he is calling me a liar! Take him away from this house. I'll see to it he never apprentices anywhere again. He doesn't deserve to learn to paint. He should spend the rest of his life cleaning stables."

"I understand your anger at his disobedience, Maestro," said my father calmly, "but it seems to me you're angry at having been discovered for what you are: a cheat. You have misrepresented yourself and have coerced these boys into lying for you. I don't condone what Arduino has done, if in fact he is guilty, but what you've done is equally contemptible. Come along, Arduino." My father picked up my bundle of things and, pulling me by the arm, led me out into the street.

Chapter Ten

I was so upset when we arrived home, I was numb. Nothing could bring me out of it: not my old dog, Nero, nor the stew my grandfather was cooking, nor my warm, soft bed. My pain was beyond tears.

I awoke the following morning to a soft knocking at my door. At first I was confused by my surroundings. Then, all in the space of a moment, I felt elation—I was back in my old room—and then grief, as the events from the previous day came back to me.

My brother Antonio came in, carrying a cup of milk.

"Here, this is warm. Drink it. You'll feel better," he said gently.

I leaned forward and took a sip. It tasted good, and I

realized how hungry I was. I emptied the cup. "I'll come down to the shop soon," I said. "As soon as I dress."

"You don't have to. Come down when you're ready."

"But Father will want me there."

Antonio took the cup from me and straightened my bedclothes.

"Don't worry," he said. "Things are under control in the shop."

"Thanks," I murmured. "I will come down later."

After he left, I got out of bed and dressed. I found my old sketch pad and pencil and headed toward the gallery window. I figured it was the only thing that might take my mind off of what had happened.

The market was as busy as ever. I looked around for a good subject for a drawing and spotted an old woman, dressed in black. A widow. She was selling eggs from a basket, and next to her was a small crate of chicks, which were also for sale. As I sketched, one of the chicks managed to hop on the edge of the crate and then down to the ground. The old woman cursed and snatched up the chick, dropping it back in the crate. I was reminded of Melania; then memories of the studio and the commission crowded my thoughts. It was no use trying to draw—I couldn't concentrate at all.

I went back to my room and lay on my bed. I recalled the events of that last day, trying to figure out where things had gone wrong.

The Maestro had accused me of telling the Duke that the sketch was not his work. I had never even spoken with the Duke. In fact, I hadn't mentioned my feelings about it to anyone.

Someone must have invented the story and lied to the Maestro. Donato? No, I was sure that he hadn't said anything. I remembered the Duke's comment: "The Maestro is a good teacher. His apprentice here is able to follow his style exactly, though he seems to add something of his own to the work." Perhaps at that moment the Duke realized the work was Donato's. But if he had gone to the Maestro about it, then he wouldn't have said that I told him anything. My name wouldn't have come up at all.

I dozed off, and Antonio woke me again as night fell.

"Arduino," he said, nudging me.

"Yes, yes." I started awake.

"Relax, nothing is happening. I brought you some rolls and honey."

I took one of the rolls, broke off a piece, and drizzled it with the honey. Antonio sat on the edge of my bed and watched me eat.

"I've been tricked, Antonio," I said in between bites. "I didn't say anything, I swear it. Someone hates me, and now I won't be able to study anywhere. No one will have me as his apprentice."

"Don't torture yourself with worry," he said. "Things will work themselves out."

But I couldn't stop worrying about it. That night, when

I was feeling more rested, I went over all the details again of my last day as the Maestro's apprentice.

I had spent the morning preparing drawings for Donato to trace with carbon on the wall.

"Tomorrow we will paint the background," Donato had said. "You will be responsible for this corner."

"Me, Maestro?"

Everyone had laughed when I called him "Maestro," except Marco, who glared at me. I recalled the Duke's visit later that day, and my conversation with Bianca. I had returned to the Maestro's after that. I remembered talking with Baldo in the studio and seeing Marco, who ran out as soon as I went in. Marco. It had to have been him. He had told the Maestro the story, out of hatred and envy.

It all fit together. Marco spoke to the Duke before leaving the palace grounds and then told the Maestro that I had betrayed him. The Maestro sent Piero to find my father, and when Donato and I returned, he sent Donato out on an errand, to keep him out of the way. Yes, it all seemed clear now, though it didn't lessen the dead feeling I had in the pit of my stomach.

I wondered whether the Duke had actually canceled the commission. He had seemed so pleased with the way things were progressing. Of course, whether it was canceled or not wouldn't affect me—the Maestro regarded me as a traitor in any case. My only hope was that Donato would tell the Maestro what had really happened. Donato knew the truth.

The next day, I helped listlessly in the kitchen and in the

tailor shop, where I sat on a low stool near a window, basting gold cord on the wide sleeves of a ceremonial doublet. When evening fell, my brothers tried to cheer me up.

"Would you like some chestnuts, Arduino? I've just roasted them."

From where he sat, Enzo held out a deck of cards.

"Would you like to play? I dare you to ten games!"

Despite their kindness, I shook my head. Nothing could relieve my despair. Even Nero tried to console me, curling up at my feet. Only my father seemed not to see me.

The next morning, I joined my grandfather in the court-yard. We sat together by the fountain. A pale sun peeked out from the clouds, painting weak shadows on the cobble-stones.

"Another spring," he said, pointing to the first buds on the branches of our almond tree.

My grandfather counted the springs. Were they the ones he had lived or the ones he had left to live? I felt an overwhelming sadness. All I had left to look forward to was counting the springs, one after another, taking my life with them.

From where we sat, we could hear some activity going on at the front of the house.

"Your father is expecting a client," my grandfather explained.

A while later, Antonio shouted to me from an open window, "Arduino, come inside—to the great room."

I looked at Grandfather. What had I done now?

He patted my back. "Go on, Arduino."

In the middle of the great room, seated in our finest chair
—the one reserved for honored guests and clients—was the
Duke of Algora. He was wearing his woolen cloak and held
a gold-headed staff in his hand. My father stood next to him.

"Arduino, the Duke has come to speak with you," he
said, beckoning me over with his hand.

I knelt before the Duke, my head bowed. "My lord, I'm
sorry—"

"Stand up, my boy," interrupted the Duke. "I'm not here
for an apology. I've spoken with Cosimo di Forlì, and it
seems that Donato needs you for the work in the chapel. As
you know, it must be finished by June."

My heart leaped. So the commission had not been canceled! I stood up slowly, my eyes still averted.

The Duke went on. "I'm aware that there was a little,
how shall I say, misunderstanding, yes, that's the word. But
fortunately, that has been cleared up. Your father and I have
discussed things, and he has agreed to allow you to return
to the studio, to help finish the chapel painting."

I couldn't believe my ears. What about the Maestro? My
father had said he would never let me go back to the studio,
but I looked at him and he nodded.

"You have my permission, Arduino," he said, softly.

Somehow, the truth had come to light. But why was my
father letting me go back? Now didn't seem the time to ask
questions.

"Father, you know this is what I want. More than anything."

"I know that, son." He came over and hugged me. "I believe you will be a wonderful painter someday."

I squeezed him tightly, then stepped back and knelt again before the Duke.

"My lord, thank you," I said. "I am deeply honored."

"Then go and gather up your things," he said. "You will return with me to the palace chapel, where your Maestro awaits you."

I think my feet hardly touched the ground on the way to my bedroom, where I hurriedly packed some clothes in my old satchel.

After a round of warm goodbyes and good wishes from my father, brothers, and grandfather, I followed the Duke out to his carriage.

There were at least a hundred questions buzzing in my head as we rode toward the palace. How had everything been resolved? How would the Maestro receive me? What about Marco? I didn't dare ask anything of the Duke—it would have been too forward—so I sat there, wondering silently, as we bounced along the cobblestone streets.

As if he were reading my thoughts, the Duke said, "I know you're curious as to how all this came about. Just wait until we get to the palace. Donato is there, and he will tell you what has transpired." He crossed his arms and in a bemused tone of voice added, "A rather unusual course of events, I should say."

. . .

When we reached the palace grounds, the Duke instructed me to go to the chapel, where I would find Donato.

I thanked him and, with satchel in hand, ran across the lawn and down the familiar path that led to the chapel. I pulled open the heavy door and looked in. For an instant, it was as if I were seeing the chapel for the first time. The spring sunlight that passed through the stained-glass windows created a vision of color.

In the back, behind the altar, was Donato, adjusting a scaffold. He hadn't heard me come in.

"Maestro!" I called. My voice echoed through the chapel.

Donato looked up from his work. "You're here!"

He hurriedly stepped over boards and other debris from painting, and I ran up to the altar. We met and embraced. Though only a few days had passed, it seemed like a lifetime since last we'd seen each other.

"Come up here," he said, pointing toward the fresco. "We have much to talk about—and much work to do."

I stopped. "Donato, tell me," I said, "it was Marco, wasn't it? He was the one who betrayed the Maestro to the Duke, then blamed it on me."

He sighed, and we both sat down on the altar step.

"Yes, it was Marco," he said. "Piero heard him tell the Maestro his lie, though at the time Piero didn't know it was a lie. He said he found it hard to believe that you would do such a thing, and knowing that you and I were friends, he came to me about it. Later, I tried to talk with the Maestro, but it was impossible. He was in a blind rage."

"Then what happened to change Cosimo's mind?" I asked.

"Well, the Duke came by the studio the next morning. He was furious with the Maestro for misrepresenting his work. When it came out that Marco was the one who had betrayed him, Cosimo was stunned. The Duke made it clear, however, that the most important thing to him was to see the chapel fresco completed for his daughter's wedding. He knew the work was mine, and because I'm in the employ of Cosimo's studio, the Duke did not cancel the commission.

"I talked to the Duke about you and how I needed your help to finish the work. I explained how you had been sent home, wrongly banished from Cosimo's studio. When I told him your name, he said he knew your father and that he would go and speak with him personally, to talk about your returning to the studio—but as my apprentice."

"What? Your apprentice? Officially? But how can it be?" I was so excited I was babbling.

Donato laughed. "Well, let me finish," he said, then paused before he went on. His voice became more serious. "As everyone now knows, Cosimo is too ill to continue running his studio. He spoke with me candidly and said he may not have long to live. Arduino, he has decided to turn the studio over to me."

"Donato, that's marvelous. You deserve it, more than anybody."

"Even if Cosimo were well enough to continue,"

Donato added, "his reputation would suffer terribly from this incident with the Duke."

"And what about Marco?" I asked.

"As you can probably guess, the Maestro gave Marco a fair hearing, then threw him out on his ear. He has gone back to his family and, I suppose, a career in the military. I feel sorry for him." Then Donato's voice brightened. "As for the others, they are all staying on."

All of them. Baldo, Piero, and Melania—and me.

The chapel door opened and the Duke strode in. Both Donato and I rose from where we sat.

"I hope you've had a chance to catch up on things," he said. "Arduino, Donato is modest, so I will tell you myself. Your future will be secure as his apprentice, because I plan to keep his studio busy for quite some time."

Donato and I looked at each other. His eyes were shining.

The Duke continued. "I would like Donato to supervise the decoration of the ceilings and walls throughout the palace," he said. Then, turning to Donato, he added, "If you agree, of course, Maestro."

"It will be my life's work, my lord."

The Duke smiled at both of us and left.

Donato turned to me. "Arduino," he said, "I have you to thank for all this good fortune. You are a brave and loyal friend."

"I was thinking the same of you, Maestro," I replied.

Later on, after several hours of painting, I went for a walk in the beautiful garden that surrounded the palace. I needed

to breathe freely and put my thoughts into order. All of the disappointments, jealousies, nightmares, and fears dissolved into an old dream, now nearly forgotten. A sweet calm filled my soul. I had an extraordinary Maestro and my father's blessing to study art. What more could I hope for?

The light of day turned violet, and the shadows softened. At the end of the stone pathway, near a door, a group of men with ropes and pulleys was lifting into place an ancient statue that had been recently restored. When I passed them, the sculptor who was directing their labors looked at me and, with a smile on his bearded face, said, "Ah, youth. What I would give to have your freedom again!"

I bowed to him, and continued back to the chapel.